Curious George®
The Kite

Adaptation by Monica Perez
Based on the TV series teleplay written by Joe Fallon

Houghton Mifflin Harcourt

For information about permission to reproduce selections from this book, write to Permissions,
Houghton Mifflin Harcourt, 215 Park Avenue South, New York, New York 10003.

Library of Congress Cataloging-in-Publication Data

Perez, Monica.
Curious George The kite / adapted by Monica Perez ; based
on the TV series teleplay written by Joe Fallon.
    p. cm.
    ISBN: 978-0-618-72396-6 (PBK)
    ISBN: 978-0-544-55373-6 (POB)
    I. Fallon, Joe. II. Title.
    PZ7.P42583Cut 2006
    2005038072

Design by Joyce White

www.hmhco.com

Manufactured in China
SCP 10 9 8 7 6 5 4 3 2 1
4500498683

It was a sunny day in the country.
George opened the window
to let in fresh cool air.

It was windy.

George liked to watch the wind
carry things away.

It carried leaves away.
It carried his cards away.
It did *not* carry his brick away.

As George looked up,
he saw something colorful in the sky.
It was a kite!

It belonged to Bill, the boy next door.
George wanted to fly the kite more
than anything in the world.

"Flying a kite is not easy," Bill said.

"But I can teach you."

Just then, his mom called,

"Billy, please come and help me!"

Bill gave George the kite string.

"Please watch my kite for me, George,"

he said. "I will be back soon."

George wanted to be good,
but he was also very curious.
He was curious about flying a kite.
George went to a field.
He held the kite up in the wind.
It began to fly away.

George chased the kite.

He chased it over a hill and past a farm.

The string pulled him along.

The wind was too strong.
It carried George away with the kite!

George was flying like a bird.

It was so much fun.

It was fun until George almost crashed

into a tree.

Now Jumpy the squirrel was flying too.
He did not like it.

Soon George was happy to see
the man with the yellow hat
flying nearby.
The man had a yellow hang glider.
He had come to take George
and Jumpy home.

George was glad to be on the
ground again.
He gave Bill the kite.
"Thanks. You are a great kite flyer!"
Bill said.
George liked flying,
but he liked walking more.

George still likes windy days.
He likes to fly kites.

He likes to fly kites that are
just the right size.

BUILD IT YOURSELF!

George likes to fly.

Don't you?

Here is how *you* can make a paper airplane of your own.

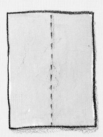

1. Fold a piece of paper in half the tall way, then unfold it again.

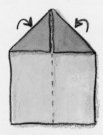

2. Fold down the top corners as shown in the picture.

3. Fold the edges in toward the crease you made in the middle.

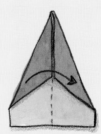

4. Now fold the plane in half and turn it to the side.

5. Make a wing from the front of the plane all the way to the back as shown in the picture.

6. You have a paper airplane!

HIGH-FLYING FUN

HOW TO FLY A KITE:

1. Fly on a day that's nicely windy. Check your local weather station—winds of 5-20 mph are best.

2. Face the direction the wind is blowing. Hold your kite straight up in the air and let the wind carry it aloft. Walk and let your line out to help the kite go higher.

3. If you have a friend with you, the friend can stand a few feet away from you and hold the kite. When your friend lets go, you can pull the string in slowly until your kite rises into the air.

4. When you're tired of flying, bring your kite down by reeling in the string and winding it around your kite spool.

DON'T
   . . . fly near telephone wires, trees, airports, or roads.
   . . . fly in rain or electrical storms.
   . . . forget to wear protective hand gear, like leather gloves.
   . . . fly near others.

DO
   . . . fly in an open field, as flat as possible.
   . . . take extra string, in case of mishaps.
   . . . add a colorful tail to your kite. It makes it easier to fly and looks great too.

Have fun!